GOD & NAOMI

Jon Ferguson

Huge Jam Publishing, 2022
www.hugejam.com

To Jacqueline Tobin for loving and resurrecting
"Three Forgotten Tales"

AUTHOR'S NOTE

This story is the third in a trilogy: *Jesus and Mary*, *Mary and God*, and now *God and Naomi*. All are about love.

At the end of *Jesus and Mary* Jesus is crucified and Mary is pregnant. Seven months later she gives birth to a child named God, hence the second book, *Mary and God*.

That book starts with the last paragraph of *Jesus and Mary*.

At the end of *Mary and God*, Mary dies. God is eighteen years old and in love with a girl named Naomi. Her fanatic Jewish father has beaten her because she refuses to marry the man he has chosen to be her husband. She runs away and takes refuge with God and Mary.

God and Naomi begins with the last chapter of *Mary and God*.

ONE

Naomi would never know if her father had looked for her or not. They never saw each other again. He would do her no more harm. In any case, she would not stay in Judea much longer.

That evening, when God and Naomi came back from the river, Mary was up and putting food on the table. She had not worried when she awoke from her sleep and found them gone. She was too tired and too weak to worry. Her only concern was setting out a few things for her son and his friend to eat. Darkness was near and she knew they would be back soon.

Mary sat with them at the table for a few minutes. They told her of their walk to the river. No, they hadn't seen anybody. Yes, Naomi's back was feeling better. Yes, they had enough to eat. No, they didn't mind if she rested while they were still eating.

Mary lay down for the last time in God's bed. God and Naomi ate, talked softly, and put things away. The large bed in the corner of the room was beckoning.

At the river they had held hands, embraced, and kissed a few times in the water. Then they dried, put their clothes back on and walked home. Now they took their clothes off for the night. Under the blanket – the same blanket Mary had had at the foot of Jesus's cross – God and Naomi fondled each other and embraced with the softest lips and the surest hands. Both were exactly where they wanted to be.

In the morning the world would have a different Pietà. God held Mary's limp body in his arms. When God and Naomi finally finished crying, Naomi stayed in the house while God went out to find Joshua and Markus. The three men would wrap Mary in her treasured blanket, carry her to the olive grove, dig a hole, and lay her in the ground.

Yes, Mary expired while God and Naomi were making love.

The next day the lovers quit Judea. There was nothing left for them in the Holy Land. Like Chaplin and Goddard at the end of *Modern Times*, arm in arm they wandered off to see the world possessing nothing more than the clothes on their backs and their love for life and each other. God did have a few coins that he had saved from making shoes, but he gave them to a blind woman as they walked past Herod's temple.

TWO

In the year 18 A. D. no one had any idea how big the earth was. Today we have a similar situation in that we don't know how big the universe is. We talk about it, throw out some big numbers, but do we really know? Modern physicists tell us that if – relatively speaking – the distance between the earth and the sun is the equivalent of the point of a pencil, then the distance from the earth to the edge of the Milky Way is from Jerusalem to New York. It's that big. But beyond that, nobody really knows how far it goes, or what is out there. God and Naomi leaving Palestine was the equivalent of two astronauts today heading straight out into space, past the moon and sun, and eventually out of our galaxy. They knew Judea, the Jews, the Romans, the Torah, and a little bit about the Greeks. But the rest of the world…? They had absolutely no idea what was out there. But they wanted to see it. Fortunately, they would live for two thousand years and hence would be able to observe quite a lot.

Like Jesus and Mary before them, God and Naomi were very curious about the world, life, and thinking. They observed how Jews and Romans differed in their beliefs about God, truth, and morality. Though they had been nurtured in a society that believed in the Old Testament, Jehovah, Moses, and the Ten Commandments, they had a hunch that there were many other ways to understand and view existence. They didn't trust the Jews, the Romans, the Bible, and especially not this man Paul who was trying to start a new religion calling God's father, Jesus, the "resurrected Son of God". In Judea they had witnessed beauty, barbarism, ingenuity, stupidity, ugliness, kindness, cruelty, savagery, tenderness, suffering, resignation, hope, hate and a few glimpses of love. Would they see more of the same as they set out to see the world? They had no idea. They just wanted to see what was out there and what was going on. And the fact that they would live for two millennia would give them an advantage over most observers of the world. The piddling thirty, fifty, seventy, or ninety years that is normally allotted to the human body and mind allows one only so much opportunity to understand existence. Of course we are all limited, but by having their terrestrial visit lengthened more than fortyfold, God and Naomi were in a good position get a decent idea of what earthly life is all about. But let's be honest…time is no guarantee of lucidity, clarity, truth, knowledge, or any such thing. As some people age their beliefs simplify and petrify, for others complexity and doubt take over. In any case, God and Naomi would stay healthy for one thousand nine hundred years. Only when the two horrendous World Wars ravaged much of the earth did their bodies begin to give out. They would die together exactly two thousand years after Jesus was born. Neither wanted to live forever anyway. Both sensed that eternity might be too long. But overall they were happy to see the sun come up 730,000 times. Today the average person experiences about twenty-five thousand sunrises.

For Naomi and God to survive so long in this world of multifarious dangers and diseases, some kind of guardian angel was necessary. Traveling in the twenty-first century is hard enough, but when God and Naomi walked out of Jerusalem there were no road signs pointing their way, no "kilometer" or "mile" numbers indicating how far it was from here to there, no passports, no smiling billboards saying "Welcome to Texas" or "You are now leaving Palestine", no real borders, no cars, no stagecoaches, no buses, taxis, trains, planes, GPSs, accurate maps, Booking.coms, or travel guides. No…back then if you wanted to go somewhere you walked on your own two feet, and if you were going very far from home you had little or no idea what to expect. Travel was often perilous, with power frequently resting in the blood-stained hands of bandits and marauders. Today's world isn't perfect, but…

So what guardian angel was watching over God and Naomi as they wandered the world? Did they have some sort of divine escort? Nah…It would have been nice, but no, God and Naomi just had each other. Their "ange gardien" was simply their unflinching abiding love for life. Everywhere they went they exuded the feeling that the simple fact of being alive was a miracle in itself. And people everywhere seemed to sense this and, hence, were generally very kind to them. People immediately intuited that God and Naomi wanted nothing from others, that they posed no danger or threat to anyone, and that they simply wanted to love each other and see – and enjoy - as much of the world as they could. They didn't want to change the people and places they visited. They looked neither up nor down at humans and civilizations. They looked the world straight in the eye and accepted it for what it was, not wishing or wanting it to be something else. It was almost as if God and Naomi were invisible. They got in nobody's way and they made no judgments about what they encountered and observed. They had no pretention of benevolence or making the world a better place. They were simply kind and respectful to every creature they encountered, human and otherwise.

That first morning they decided to walk north, never straying too far from the great blue sea. There was something about its openness, vastness, and mystery that was like a spark in their guts. For months they walked up and down arid hills and plains and along beaches. "Which is bigger," Naomi once asked, "the land, the sea, or the sky?" God answered with a question, "Do you think any of them end?"

One day they came upon a fertile river that emptied into the sea. They followed it eastward where they saw many Roman soldiers and masses of slaves building walls and working the land. They were near the great city of Damascus that they had heard about in the Bible. They stayed for a few days watching the bustle of humanity. "Why do people do what they do and not other 'things'?" God said one afternoon. Naomi didn't answer. She was thinking of all the pain women had endured giving birth to all the human beings passing before her eyes. She had never had a child herself, but her mother had told her how she had not cared if she lived or died as her babies were struggling to leave her womb and see the world. As she was lost in her thoughts, God said, "I watch birds blithely cruising and darting through the sky...I see men slaving under the burning sun and wonder if I should cry..."

They went back to the sea and eventually their path turned in the direction of the cooling sun. They chatted with an old man tending sheep who told them that if they kept walking, they would find the rich and wonderful Hellenic kingdom, though he wasn't sure how long it would take for them to get there. He thought less than a year.

He was right. After a hundred days of ambling in relative solitude, they came upon a coterie of Roman soldiers who told them that if they kept on, in three days' time they would be able to see the Acropolis, "a building as beautiful as anything in Rome".

God and Naomi arrived in Greece long before Christianity did. They decided to settle down for a while, rest their bodies, and learn a new language. They were given a room in a small house owned by a man named Epictetus. He showed them the Acropolis and explained how the Athenian community was organized. It made God wonder if this "Zeus" creature he kept hearing about might actually be for real. "How could men build such a building?" he remarked to Naomi. "How can people be so civilized?" she replied, and added that she wasn't sure which surprised her more…man's goodness or his barbarity. (She still had scars on her back from the beatings her father had inflicted upon her when she refused to marry the Jewish man he had chosen for her.)

Within months Naomi and God were able to understand and converse with the locals in the marketplace. Epictetus helped them by saying, "Languages are not difficult to learn. Three-year-olds can speak them all. You just have to bathe in them and they will sink into your skin."

God and Naomi noticed there was much more "intellectual" discussion among the people in Hellas than there had been back in Palestine. In Palestine things were rather straightforward: the Jews followed the rabbis, the rabbis followed the Torah, and the Romans took care of governing the place. People didn't spend a lot of time worrying about metaphysical and moral questions. They were much like people today who want to have a nice house, a nice car, a big television, watch football games, have a few beers, and when it's over, go to heaven. The rest just doesn't mean too much. In Hellas things were different. Epictetus himself had been a slave in Rome and had been banished from the city by an emperor who "hated all philosophers". He reflected constantly and insisted that people should not worry about what they can't control. "Don't grieve over spilled milk because it's already been spilled and there is absolutely nothing you can do about it except clean up the mess." He talked softly and walked gently, but he was a firm supporter of Zeus, "whose fiery breath had organized all life." He told Naomi and God that, "We should accept Zeus's desires as the world is unfolding according to His wishes." He also gave consummate thanks to Zeus for everything because, "In the end everything belongs to Him." This amused God and Naomi as in many ways it reminded them of the people back in Palestine. Zeus and Jehovah had much in common, but neither Naomi nor God could see a reason to believe one was real and the other wasn't. How the world got here and who owned it and watched over it remained an enigma. For them, neither Jehovah not Zeus provided a sufficient answer.

They spent some of their last days in Hellas watching and listening to architects, fascinated as they were by the Greek capacity to build. God said, "If I were running the world there wouldn't be any houses and everybody would be sleeping under the stars or in caves. I have no idea how to build such structures. It's a good thing I'm not running the world." Naomi smiled and said, "But if you were running the world there wouldn't be any slaves sweating in unbearable heat." She kissed him and God wondered if she might be right.

They stayed in the Greek world from summer to spring. The weather had been almost as warm as it was in Judea and the people went about their daily lives with a certain calm and serenity. They saw many babies born and many people die. They heard much talk about the cosmos, politics, morality, and what constituted a noble life. God often thought that, given what his mother had told him about Jesus, the father he never met would probably have liked these people. They noticed how the Hellenes treated their dead with great respect and how they believed that when a person died, his or her "spirit" immediately left the body like a puff of air or wind. Of course, no one could see this "spirit" as it was released from the lifeless body, but it seemed to be an idea that Greek people took to easily and with gusto. God wondered if Paul had heard about it, Paul who had begun preaching that Jesus had been "resurrected" and gone to heaven to live with His Father…not only his spirit, but also his body. He remembered the morning when he held death in his arms – his mother Mary - and how her inert cooling body had felt.

God and Naomi pondered many questions, and answers were like greasy snakes.

Before they left the Greek world, Epictetus gave them a lovely blue blanket on which they slept a few evenings outside in an olive grove. "Let us thank Zeus for this soft blanket," Naomi whispered on their last night. "And for the umbrella of stars," God added before they commenced making love. "O what a world," Naomi said as their bodies began to become one.

THREE

For twenty years they wandered continuously to the north and east. The air got colder and for many days the sun would never rise very high in the sky. They encountered countless new faces and human forms and colors. Eyes and hair were different. Skin was different. Clothes were thick. Animals were killed, the skins of which were used to keep the human beings warm. "People are so different, yet so similar," God said one day. "We keep walking and eventually we always find more people. No one seems to know how they got to be where they are." "Most were born quite near to where they are now," Naomi said. "I don't think many other people have walked as far or have seen as much of the world as we have." "Could the world be never ending? "I don't know." "Why do you think we or anything else lives?" "I don't know." "It seems people have many different reasons for living." "I think most people are like animals…they don't think about 'why' they live…they just live." "And then die…" "I think I live to love you." "Why do we love?" "That I know…Without our love, life would be as empty as the space between the moon and the sun." "Do you think there is only one sun and one moon?" "It is possible, but I don't know for sure." "What do you mean?" "I mean every day we see the sun…Is it always the same sun? Or does it have brothers and sisters and they take turns visiting us? The same for the moon. It often looks different. Maybe there are many moons dancing around us…" "But we never see more than one at a time." "Yes, it makes me wonder."

They finally started moving south where they were quite sure the weather would be warmer. How did they know this? How do birds know it? They sensed they should settle down again soon and they wanted to do it in a clement climate. When they had been far to the north where for months at a time it was very cold and the sun very low, they wondered why people lived in such places. Maybe they didn't know other parts of the world were warmer. God and Naomi had tried to explain to people that there were places on the earth where the weather was very pleasant. But the people just laughed. For them there was nothing wrong with their weather. In any case, God and Naomi didn't stay long enough in these cold areas to learn the local language well. Perhaps the people simply never understood what they were trying to say.

After many years of wandering through mountains and valleys, the world started to become warmer and greener. They even began to see elephants, monkeys, strange snakes, and spiders the size of human hands. "Where do you think these creatures come from?" God asked one day. "Where does anything come from?" Naomi responded. "With every passing day the world becomes odder and odder." "I thought it would become less mysterious. But the opposite is happening." "Yes, my love."

One very warm and muggy afternoon after a torrential rain had left them wet to the bone, they were taken into a home and given food and dry clothes by a kind woman. There was no man in the house, but the woman had many children and cats. "Where are we on this earth?" they asked her gesturing with their hands and eyes. "Nan…Yang…" she said. Of course they had no idea where they were or what she meant. But they liked where they were and the woman seemed happy to have them around. They decided to stay for a while and built a little hut with palm branches next to the woman's home. They lived there for more than a decade, until all the original cats had died. But more were born. They learned the language and watched the children grow into adulthood. Some died, some had babies. The village grew.

One evening God and Naomi wandered to a river upon which a large yellow moon was shining.

"There must be more than one moon. It's not possible it can be so different from one place to another…" "I don't know." "Why does it always look bigger when it is low and near to the earth and smaller when it is high in the sky?" "How do you know when it is near or far? Maybe one moon is very big and far away and another is very small and close to the earth? Just because something is near to the eye does not make it big, even though it looks that way." "Of course." "Do you remember that white-tusked animal that we saw the other day. At first it looked small and then as we moved closer it revealed itself to be bigger than any animal we had ever seen." "There are so many things we don't know. When people say the moons are bigger than the stars I have to doubt them. When they say the heavens move, but earth stays still, I have to doubt them. Earth? Heavens? Where is the center?" "Why do people think there is a center?" "Do you think we are at the center?… Maybe there is no center." "I don't know. When I take the time to think on any subject, I always begin to doubt myself. If I'm honest, the only thing I really know is that I love you." "You're such a silly beast, dear God! You sound like those monkeys that were flying through the trees and laughing at us yesterday." "They looked happy… happier than most people we meet." "What do most people have to be happy about?" "I don't know…life…and monkeys?" "What do monkeys have to be happy about?" "I wonder why the air is so different here? It is like another layer of skin, creamy and heavy, even when there are no clouds or rain falling from the sky." "Do you think the rain makes the clouds or do the clouds make the rain?" "I don't know. Sometimes there are many clouds and no rain." "Does the rain only come down from the clouds or might it go up too…in the other direction…away from the earth?" "I don't know. Only birds that fly above the clouds can know such a thing. I wonder if there are birds flying all through the heavens?" "Where do you think the heavens stop?" "Oh God, how many millions of questions can we ask? Why is it that other people don't seem to ask questions like you and I do?" "I think they are too busy living to ask such questions. Do monkeys and elephants ask questions?" "Another good question." "With no answer." "In any case, I think I like questions better than answers. Questions open doors. Answers close them." "Look how green everything is here. Why is there so much more rain here than in Palestine?" "I don't know… Don't you think the people here are beautiful? I love the shape of their eyes." "At first they looked strange…like everything else new… People here looked as if they were ready to sleep all the time…Now that I'm used to them, I love them…It's your oval eyes that look strange!" "These people seem to have more energy than people whose eyes stay wide open." "To them I'm sure our eyes seem as though there is something wrong with the lids." "Is it not odd how people always think their world is the 'normal' world?" "It is not odd; it is the most human of all things. We've seen it everywhere. The world always starts with oneself and one's people. Whatever is not like 'us' is always considered strange." "Have you noticed that the people here never talk about either Jehovah or Zeus?" "It is true…I've have never heard the words 'Zeus' or 'Jehovah'. They speak of different forces behind the world. I'm not sure if they're speaking of gods, but I often hear the word 'Tao'." "It seems to be the name of someone or something they care about very much. But I'm never exactly sure of the meaning of what they are saying. Languages are slippery fish." "It's interesting that everywhere we go, young children understand a language far better than we do." "Are we all born with the language of our parents in our heads?" "I don't know. We might be. Two-year-olds know little about anything, but they can talk…" "We can't remember what was happening when we were two years old, so we don't know how we learned to speak." "Remember the other evening when we tried to tell the woman what Palestine was like. I told her about the Jews, Jehovah, and how the Hebrew people believe the world was 'created'. She thought it was funny to think that the world had been 'created'." "I've been thinking about that. These people don't seem to believe that the world was made by a god. They think it has always been here." "And me…I've been thinking about my father when he used to beat me and scream about 'Jehovah' and my 'sins'. Since we left Hellas the word 'Jehovah' has no meaning for anybody and I've never heard anyone talking about 'sin'." "Yes, it is a strange world, and like you said the other day, the more we see the stranger it gets." "People here are so gentle and calm. They don't talk about having gold or wanting to get rich. They don't speak about hell or heaven. Here people would think my father was completely crazy for beating me. My father would think these people are all going to hell because none of them believes in Jehovah." "They've never heard of Jehovah…Did you hear the old man yesterday in the market talking about the Tru'ng sisters?" "A little bit. They were his heroes. Sisters…women." "In Palestine all the heroes are gods or men." "Yes…He said the sisters led a rebellion against the attackers from the north that had come down to control their people. The people from the north wanted them to dress and talk like they did. But the Tru'ang sisters said "NO!" and rallied the people against the invaders." "Why would the people from the north want to impose their way of life on others?" "Because they're human…" "Did you understand the end of the story about the sisters?" "No, I don't remember. What happened?" "The people from the north trapped them in some cave or building or something. They were going to kill the sisters, but the sisters wouldn't let them because they killed themselves first." "Don't you hate the world sometimes?" "Remember what that Greek Epictetus said about not worrying about things you can't control." "Yes, it is good advice." "It seems that people here are a little less crazy than the people back home. Not all of them, but most of them." "Do you want to stay here longer or shall we move on?" "If we go away, I will need some new shoes." "I will make you some. Remember, when we met I was a shoemaker." "And I was a sad child." "We've come a long way, my love." "Yes, but hasn't our voyage just begun?"

FOUR

God made the shoes. They left that part of the world and wandered for a long time through what is now China and Mongolia. They saw millions die of pestilence, hunger, cold, war, and disease. They saw thousands of mothers lose life at birth - their babies' and their own. They watched the human race struggle to survive another day, another year, another decade. When one sees so much suffering and death, there is an inevitable numbing of the mind and heart, but God and Naomi tried to feel compassion and love for every creature they encountered everywhere they went. Life was a miracle and they were part of it. But they often wondered where the limits were as to what the human spirit could endure? Was there enough joy to balance the pain? In any case, they lived on – century after century – while everyone around them perished. They saw thousands and thousands of bodies go back into the earth and many others rot away in lonely nooks and crannies, or get eaten by other forms of life.

They began to learn languages more quickly. They became fascinated by the similarities and variations from one region to the next. How old were these languages? How did they all come to be? Who made the rules? Some were written down and others were not... Why? Who created the signs and symbols? One thing was certain: humans everywhere talked and humans everywhere used language to get things done and to tie themselves together in one way or another.

God and Naomi were there for what history calls "the Jin dynasty". They cringed as civil wars unfolded and the vicious struggle for power sent so many young men to their graves. They heard wise old sages again talking about the "Tao", the yin and the yang, and even how the human body was a reflection of the cosmos. God asked, "Why our bodies, and not the bodies of birds, snakes, or sheep?" And Naomi answered, "Because man is man..."

Little by little they made a huge loop and finally headed back in the direction of the setting sun. Three hundred years had passed since they left Palestine when they arrived in the large metropolis of Constantinople. God was in for a shock: there were churches everywhere and countless representations of his father. He and Naomi had pretty much forgotten about the religion that Jesus's friend Paul had started after Jesus had died. And now, there it was, burning like a fire in the hearts of an enormous mass of people. Long-robed, thick-bearded Christian priests were everywhere all claiming to be "men of God". When God told them his name was "God" they scoffed and said calling oneself "God" was heretical. When God calmly replied that Jesus was his father and had chosen the name "God" for his only son, they all thought God was a madman and some even took pity on him. One of these holy men sat God and Naomi down and showed them a book, *The New Testament*, that was said to contain all the teachings of Jesus. God wondered where whoever wrote the book got his or her information. Mary had told God all about his father's life and little or nothing in the book corresponded to anything she had said, except that Jesus was a very kind man and that he died on a wooden cross. But the rest...the virgin mother, the miracles, the resurrection, the kingdom of heaven, the spirit of god, sin, angels – none of this had anything to do with what Mary had said about the love of her life.

The longer God stayed in Constantinople the more he was saddened by what the men in the long robes were saying. One day he met one such priest on the street and they had this conversation ...

Sir, I know you don't believe me when I say I am the son of Jesus, but let me tell you what my mother said about my father. You must understand that I never knew him because he died before I was born. But I knew well the woman with whom Jesus made love to make me – the woman named Mary Magdalene whom he loved to death.

Stop talking foolishness my friend.

I am not talking foolishness. You and the other priests are the ones who are talking nonsense. You know nothing about the real Jesus.

It saddens me to hear you say such a thing. Yet this priest was open-minded and wanted to hear God out. *Tell me what you think you know about our Lord and Savior Jesus Christ.*

I thank you for at least listening to me, kind sir. The other men in the long robes all lend nary an ear to listen to anything I have to say.

So what kinds of things did your mother tell you?

What she told me most was that Jesus was absolutely fascinated by everything that existed. He thought life was a profound mystery.

Only God knows the truth of the world.

What god? Which god? My mother said Jesus did not know which god to believe in. He looked at the Jewish God and the Greek and Roman Gods and said there was no reason to think any of them were real. That's why he wanted to name me "God"… because then he would know for sure that there was at least one real God.

God laughed when he said this, but the priest didn't.

Perhaps you are the son of Jesus, but Jesus was the

Son of God.

My father never said he was the son of any divinity. He said he was the son of a man called Joseph and woman named Mary. It was his so-called friend Paul who said Jesus was the Son of God. Jesus himself never said such a thing.

Paul was a prophet. He was a disciple of Jesus Christ. Jesus Christ is our Lord. Jesus Christ was the Son of God and He is our Savior.

Jesus never said any of these things. It was the man Paul who made all these wild proclamations after my father had died.

They are not wild proclamations. They are the truth, the truth that is between the pages of the Holy Bible. Not only was Jesus born of the Virgin Mary, but He died for the sins of the world…for my sins and your sins and the sins of all mankind.

Jesus never talked about sin. My mother told me many times that, if anything, Jesus thought men were not that different from all the other creatures that roam the earth. He said all creatures were strange, all were a mystery, and no one knew why any were what they were and acted the way they acted. My mother said Jesus never used the word "sin" to describe what men did.

But don't you know that hell is for the world's sinners and heaven is for those who follow the Word of God. And Jesus gave us the Word of God in the New Testament.

Jesus never spoke about a heaven or a hell. He never spoke about a God in heaven or a Devil in hell. He only talked about this life and trying to make it as livable as possible. All he wanted to do was minimize suffering and help people to treat each other with respect and dignity.

Who was your mother?

Mary Magdalene.

Mary Magdalene was a harlot. Jesus never made love to her or to any other woman. Jesus was pure and without sin.

Why was making love to my mother a sin? They loved each other more than any man and woman have loved. God smiled and said, *At least that's what my mother told me.*

If Jesus had had a child, that child would have been born of a virgin, just like Jesus was. I am sorry to tell you that if Mary Magdalene was your mother, she was the opposite of Jesus's mother. She was a whore, a sinner and a fornicator. But how can she be your mother? She died three hundred years ago!

I should be angry with you for saying such things. But I am not the son of Jesus for nothing. Just let me say that you have no idea what you're talking about. None of you priests does. But it is not your fault. If anything, that is what Jesus – my father – taught the world. He said that stupidity is never anybody's fault. Nobody wants to be stupid. Stupidity is simply part of the world, like disease, suffering, pain, and death. You cannot help being what you are. You cannot help being so misinformed. I cannot expect you to believe that I am the son of Jesus and Mary Magdalene and that I am three hundred years old. But you should at least listen to me when I tell you that my mother loved Jesus more than any woman has ever loved a man, and Jesus loved her more than any man has ever loved a woman, and that I, God, am the fruit of their love. I am the fruit of the greatest lovemaking ever. God rubbed his belly and chest.

The priest flew into a rage and shouted… *You are deranged! You are evil! You are a blasphemer! You don't know who you are! Jesus died three hundred years ago. He was resurrected and you too will be resurrected, but you will go to hell! … Eternally damned for your blasphemy!*

God remained as calm as the morning sea…

From where do you get your idea of eternal life? From that Bible of yours? From that man Paul who told nothing but lies about my father? Yes, I am three hundred years old. But the last thing I want is to live eternally. Naomi and I just want to see as much of this world as possible. Fortunately we live longer than other people. We have seen a lot and we hope to see much more. But one day I am sure that Naomi and I will have had enough living. Then we will want to die.

The priest stepped back away from God and screamed, *The man you claim to be your father was crucified to save mankind! And you do not even want to be saved! You do not want Eternal Salvation! You do not want to be part of His sacrifice! If you are anything, you are the son of the Devil, not the son of Jesus Christ!* The priest moved toward God menacingly, his clenched teeth showing through his beard. But he did not strike him. God looked him in the eye, and then spoke in a near whisper…

My dear sir, I understand why you believe all that you believe about this life. I understand how you have been taken in by all the teachings and beliefs of your culture and civilization. Everywhere Naomi and I have traveled we have seen the same thing. People follow the traditions of their ancestors. You have your so-called "Christian" tradition. It has spread like a fire in a forest. You have your Bible, your churches, and your long robes. But my friend, you don't have the truth. No one does. This is what my father taught. No man knows the truth about the mystery of life. My father never talked about a god. He didn't talk about life after death. He believed in this life, here and now. He believed in the earth, nothing more. We don't know where the earth begins and ends, but at least we know we walk on it. We eat and sleep and love. Some of us hate. But this earth is not some wishful eternity…some hoped-for afterlife. For Jesus, 'this life' was sacred. He claimed no knowledge about any other life or kingdom. He tried to understand people. He tried to be kind to people. He tried to make the earth as livable as possible for all people he met. That is all. God paused.

The priest glared at him but said nothing. Finally God said softly, *I will leave you now. My love and I are going to continue our journey, farther in the direction of the setting sun. Goodbye my friend...*

FIVE

The Christian religion had, in fact, spread like a wildfire. It started in Rome and had taken hold of the hearts and minds of millions of people across that part of the world. It was squeezing human brains. It was shrinking them. It was telling them its way was the only way, that its truth was the only truth. God saw it as a disease of the mind and even the body as many of the stone-faced priests began insisting that the human body was somehow unclean, even evil, and that only the spirit counted. God knew from his mother Mary that Jesus had never separated the mind from the body, that the love of her life had appreciated the body and mind equally, and in fact, that he had never made a distinction between the two. Of this God was sure. And now when he saw priests bellowing about how the flesh was wicked, God was saddened that his father's life was being used in such a manner. But as he and Naomi walked on, they knew it was too late. There were churches, crosses, and images of Jesus everywhere. God remembered what Epictetus said about not worrying about things you can't control. But what sorrowed them even more was that people were fighting – even killing each other – as they argued about what Jesus *really* said and taught, when, in fact, none of them had any idea what had actually come from Jesus's mouth and heart. "Jesus said that"…"Jehovah commands this"… "Do this and you will go to heaven"… "Do that and you will burn in hell!" – the priests exhorted the masses. It was a farce beyond measure. But Naomi and God knew there was no stopping it. Even Jesus's mother got taken through the wash and had come out bleached as the whitest virgin to walk the face of the earth. Yes, God's family tree had been uprooted forever.

There was, however, one thing that some of the priests were saying that did have a few grains of truth to it: "Father forgive them for they know not what they do". Now that part of the Bible was true! Jesus *had* said that! And he would have forgiven those misguided priests for all the other nonsense they were spreading. Why? Because Jesus forgave everybody. Why? Because the whole universe was innocent. Everything…absolutely everything was innocent. Nothing asked to be what it was. No moon, no bug, no bee, no tree, no star, no man....not even the long-robed men with the granite faces. "The world," God said as he and Naomi walked slowly westward, "is deeper than anyone knows…far, far deeper than any human mind will ever go."

SIX

For the next two hundred years God and Naomi wandered through the areas now referred to as Asia Minor, the Middle East, and Northern Africa. They saw that another religion was spreading – a new fire. It – Islam – had many similarities with the Christian religion that was already rampant: there is only one God (not Jehovah, but Allah), hell and heaven are as real as the sun and the moon, do what the prophet says and the virgins will be waiting for you, go against the prophet's teachings and you're in for a rough life and eternity!… Yes, two blazes were burning the minds of the people they came in contact with. Even the Greeks were talking that way.

God and Naomi just sighed…and observed. One morning when they awoke in the sand next to the creaseless sea, God said, "Naomi, I don't know what I would do without you." "I feel the same way about you God." "What a world this is!... O what a curious world." "Everywhere we go now one of these two religions is taking over people's minds." "Yes, it is as if there are no other ways to see the world, life, and the universe." "People's minds are rather simple and stale here. We must keep walking and look for new ideas and fresh air. There must be other parts of the earth where people see things differently…like where we were with the woman and her many cats and children." "Yes…but here, in this part of the world, I am beginning to wonder. I hope we can find other populations with other visions of life. It is true that many of these people are very kind, but their minds are petty and small. I know it's not their fault. But I would just as soon talk to sheep as to them." "They are sheep. Sheep with a different bleat. It is amazing how they are satisfied with such silly stories to explain the great mystery of life. It is as if they live like worms underground and never come up to see any light. Their heads are always in the thick dirt that covers the earth. And then to see them pray on their knees, with their eyes closed – what a sight it is! One would think they would pray standing up with their arms raised to the sun…to light…to the open skies!" "O what a world … People are beggars satisfied with a few simple answers to the deepest questions." "But perhaps the deepest questions have no answers." "That is very possible, my love. If there is comfort in these religions, it is understandable how the gentle herds will flock to them. They will chew on whatever keeps them alive...now and forever..." Naomi took God's wrist and kissed his sun-browned arm. "Maybe that is why your parents named you 'God'... They wanted people to feel divinity every time they saw you." "The only divinity they knew was their love for each other. I was the fruit of that love. I was the God of Love." "And my parents were the opposite of yours. They knew no love of anything. They feared everything. They feared the rabbis. They feared the Romans. They feared hell and damnation. They feared I would marry a man that was not a man of God...their god Jehovah. Little did they know that I found the one true God...my one true love." Naomi laughed and rolled on top of God.

Later they went for a swim in the sea that was melted into the azure sky.

SEVEN

They headed farther south. Much to their surprise and curiosity, they began to encounter humans who had skin of a different color. Naomi and God hoped that these people's minds and ideas about life would be different as well. Their scantily clad bodies were various shades of brown and black, with little tints of purple depending on the light of the sun. They noticed that their hands and tongues were pink like those of the people up north. Many had long sleek bodies and they were a pleasant change from human beings they were used to seeing. God wondered if their blood was blackish, too, but then he remembered that his own blood wasn't the same color as his skin and that sheep and pigs had blood very similar to his. Was rich red blood common to all living creatures? – They got their answer a few days later when they met a young woman who was in the middle of giving birth. They stopped to help her and when the small black head began to poke out of the woman's womb, they saw that her blood was the same color as theirs. And then when they encountered men with spears and knives warring with each other, again they saw thin rivers of crimson liquid leaking from the bodies of men and animals. *How does blood get into bodies?* they wondered. *Men, women, children and animals all have it and it is always the same sparkling red. Why does death occur when large quantities leak from the body? Is blood the juice of life?* …And God remembered what his mother had told him about how she was alone beneath the cross when Jesus died and how the last drops of his blood fell onto her face…

On they walked, closely observing these new people. They were excited to learn their language in order to understand what they thought and how they saw the world, but they soon realized that each group they met spoke a different tongue. Interestingly, after months of walking they hadn't seen a single church or cross, nor had they heard Jesus's name mentioned once. They were happy and relieved that the lies about God's father and mother had not spread to this part of the world. "Perhaps these people sing a different song about what existence was all about," Naomi said one day. "Let us hope so," God said, "and let us hope that that they are happier with this world than those who speak of Allah and Jehovah and sin and fire."

After wandering for a few weeks, they were invited to settle in a place where a river ran into a large lake. They stayed for ten years – a long time for some, a puff of smoke in the imagination for others.

In general, the people were very kind. They lived simply and built fewer buildings than the humans they had known in the north. But because the air was warmer, they didn't need as much protection from the weather. What fascinated God and Naomi was that though these people were different in many ways, they still had much in common with the creatures they met throughout their travels. They wondered if there was such a thing as "the human type"? Were all men and women of the same family, like all rabbits or all cats or dogs? But maybe, they thought, this way of grouping creatures was completely mistaken... Was each creature unique and to be considered as such? Or, inversely, should ALL living creatures be grouped together in ONE family of the living?

God and Naomi had no answers. But they had the questions.

One day they had this conversation:

You know, Naomi, at first I thought these people would be very different from the people of Palestine, Greece, Rome, China, Mongolia, and Vietnam. They were a different color. Many were bigger and stronger. But in the end they are so similar. They too have explanations for where everything came from. They believe in a creator. They have a vision of right and wrong, good and bad, real and unreal. They talk about "spirits" and souls departing from bodies. They talk about life after death. They sometimes sacrifice animals to their divinities…

Yes, God. I have thought the same. When I look into their dark eyes I see the same hopes and fears…

Do you see these hopes and fears when you look into the eyes of a camel or a lamb?

Yes, when the lamb is ready to be slaughtered or when the camel is weary from walking.

Why do we differentiate so between men and animals?

I don't know. I have thought much about this. All creatures are mysteries and wonders of the world. All have eyes, hearts and blood. On what basis do we value some more than others?

It seems that human beings everywhere value certain creatures more than others. But which creatures are valued changes from place to place.

Can any man or woman say "why" he or she values one thing over another?

Most people value what keeps them alive. Then they value what their traditions have passed on to them. Then they value what is rare and beautiful in their eyes.

And beauty changes from one place to another.

As does the weather, the faces, the clothes, the

sounds that come from mouths, what they eat, and the gods they worship.

Can any man or woman truly explain why they do what they do? Here they chant, dance, and beat on drums in the open air. Why? In the north we saw them praying on their knees in cold churches. Why?...Why?...Why?

It seems that nobody ever looks into their own soul and truly asks why they do what they do, why they think what they think, why they say what they say, and why they believe what they believe.

Maybe only the gods do that...

I doubt it. The gods are too busy creating universes and judging their creatures. (They laugh and kiss.)

Sometimes I think the idea of a god is the silliest idea ever to pass through a human head...Imagine thinking the universe was created... What an idea...! What a silly idea! Just because men create houses, boats, and buildings doesn't mean that everything was created. If a creator created the world, who – or what – created the creator? Such an idea always just begs the question. In any case, human beings always see the world through the eyes of human beings. Fish see the world through the eyes of fish. If there are gods, they see the world through the eyes of gods...

The deepest questions can never be answered... Never... This is what I think I have learned so far in life.

I know. I look into the bottom of my heart to try to understand why I love what I love. I have asked myself a thousand times why I love you and only you. And of course I can never explain it. If I can't explain what is the closest and dearest to me, how can I expect to explain something outside of myself?

You can't…we can't.

And how can anyone expect to explain someone else's behavior? Or an animal's behavior?

Here, in this part of the world, I am so amused at how the shamans tell people what is causing what and what people should and shouldn't do. And the people are satisfied. People everywhere are satisfied with answers from those who "are supposed to know". In the north it was the priests. When we were children it was the rabbis with their bibles and Romans with their whips.

I believe no one. Everywhere we go I see the blind following the blind.

Everywhere we go there are people who are supposed to know more than others…people who are supposed to have the secrets to life's questions and dilemmas. It is fascinating how their followers believe them.

It is the human way. It is what we see everywhere… some have the power and others bow down to it. Some claim to have knowledge and the others acquiesce.

It is interesting how sometimes the powerful are gentler in some places than in others.

Here they have taken us in with open arms. They were not afraid of us.

They have been kind. Saying goodbye will not be easy.

Can you imagine the day we say goodbye to life.

I have tried many times to imagine it. I think that as I breathe my last breath I will whisper, "What was that?"

Yes, life is such a mystery.

The only thing I know is that I want to breathe my last breath with you, my darling. Love is when life does not make sense without the other.

Does it ever make sense?

Only in the life of love…

After ten years, God and Naomi said goodbye to their dark-skinned friends and headed back up north. When they met pale faces again they seemed very odd, as did the smaller noses and lips, and the straight hair that dropped down on their shoulders. But little by little, their minds and eyes adjusted. Soon the Caucasian type looked normal again.

EIGHT

As they wandered, they wondered how much more world there was to see. One morning, after many years of walking in the direction of the setting sun, they came upon a vast beach. They stood and stared at the incessant waves. The water continuously flowed toward them, lapping the shore, then disappearing back into the motherly sea. They had a bit of food and water, so they sat and ate. Their eyes saw only sand, water, a long flat line, and blue sky. There was nothing else…absolutely nothing else.

What could be out there? Naomi asked. *Could there be more land? Could there be more creatures similar to what we have seen?*

I don't know. If there are more creatures, I think I would be more interested in their minds than their bodies. We have seen many fascinating people and animals. Sometimes the animals are more fascinating than the people... They both thought of the lions, giraffes, hippos, rhinos, monkeys, birds, cheetahs, antelopes, and gorillas that they had seen living near their dark-skinned friends... There might be more amazing creatures somewhere. But what I'd like to see are some amazing minds...minds that turn the world inside out...minds that have not been put to sleep by the traditions around them, minds that do not see the world around them as "normal" and commonplace, but who see mystery, tragedy, beauty, and infinity...in everything! It is sad how so many human beings are so lacking in curiosity and wonder. Many, If not most, are no more curious than the cows that were eating grass all day in the fields we have just crossed before arriving here at this beach.

I don't know if it is sad. Is being a cow a sad thing? Perhaps simplicity is a good thing for most creatures. Too much complexity might be bad for them, just like it might be bad for many human minds.

You might be right, my love. I don't know why I always expect humans to be something other than what they are. It is a silly prejudice I have. I don't do it for monkeys and sheep and cows... so why should I do it for people?

You just always hope people will be better. You want the best for everybody and every creature, from the largest to the smallest. You are not Jesus's son for nothing.

And you are not my love for nothing…You know Naomi, human beings might be some of the best creatures, but they are also some of the worst. They are the only creatures that kill for a god they have never seen or heard speak. They seem to be the only creatures that kill without wanting to eat what they kill. They can kill for land and power and leave the dead lying on the field of battle. Is anything more barbaric than that? I can't help wanting them to be less cruel and stupid. You never see a butterfly or a sheep causing harm to another creature. Few animals are cruel. They are usually only cruel when they are trying to protect themselves. Man can be cruel for many other reasons. It is that that I hope will change.

But it is very possible that man will never change.

Yes, it is…Why should he change? What part of him might make him change? Don't most men think that how they live and how they think makes perfect sense…to them?

They were silent for a long while. The sun dropped toward the empty horizon. They watched it disappear and marveled again at the colors that appeared in the sky – stripes of red, orange, yellow, violet, and blue. Then slowly the water and sky darkened and stars filled the black above them. They lay down on the blanket on the sand. When God said, *I want to find a way to go out on the water and see what is there,* Naomi didn't hear him. She was already asleep. Her lovely legs and mind had walked many miles that day.

NINE

For years and years they wandered up and down the coast, but they met no one who had found a way to explore the vast sea stretching endlessly toward the setting sun. People seemed to fear what was out there, fear how far it went, and fear that anyone who ventured forth would eventually fall off and drop into the depths of space. God was not so sure. He once held an apple in his hand and ran his finger around its smooth skin. It came back to the place it had started. From that moment onward he wondered if the world might be shaped like the apple. Was the sun flat? Was the moon flat? The apple wasn't flat? Perhaps sun, moon, and earth were as round as apples!

Of course God was not the only one who had had this thought. But such thinkers were few and not met.

In the meantime, God and Naomi had begun hearing rumors that in the other direction – in the direction of the rising sun – people were massacring each other in great numbers in God's name and Jesus's name. God was deeply saddened and wondered anew how man could be such a cruel beastly creature.

Really, Naomi, why do you think they do such things? God asked one morning as they walked in the sand under a warming sun.

The same answer always comes into my mind…Why does any creature behave the way it does at any moment? Who can say? Who can understand? Who can know? Sometimes I think that any question beginning with "why" is a ridiculous one? Why is the sky blue? Why is this beach here and not over there? Why water here and not there? Why do we ask our questions? Why do people everywhere invent gods? Why do we even think? Why do we feel joy and pain? Why do people kill each other in the name of their divinities? Every answer just begs another question. In the end there are no answers. Both the questions and answers can go on forever. There is no solace when one takes the mind in such a direction.

Yes, my darling, and that is why I look to love for solace. It is the only place where my mind stops and is at peace. Otherwise it just keeps digging deeper and the hole keeps getting bigger.

I know, dear God, but we too are human and we

too have minds and bodies that we can't always control.

They were alone. They removed their clothes and made love in the sand.

What they had heard about the people slaughtering each other was not just rumor. The Christians were killing the Jews and Muslims who did not agree with their view of life and the world. The stone-faced men in the long robes were sending out armies in the name of God to cleanse the earth of the so-called "infidels". *They're all infidels,* God thought. *They abuse my father's life, my name, and worst of all, they abuse life on this earth. They are all worms with their heads in the ground.*

Fortunately the day God had been waiting for came. One morning as he and Naomi were strolling near the sea, they saw a throng of men building an enormous boat. They approached the site and questioned the man who was shouting orders and seemed the leader…

What are you planning to do with this beautiful vessel?

We want to see if there is an end to the ocean. We want to see if there are other lands and people out there. Some men are saying the earth is round like an orange and that if we keep going we can come back to where we started.

What do you think, my good man?

The man looked at God's gentle face and wondered if he had ever seen such eyes of empathy and compassion. *I don't know*, he said. *But I want to find out.*

I share your questions and your ideas, God said. *I once held an apple and thought maybe the earth was shaped like fruit. You think it might be like an orange.*

In any case, it is a mystery and I want to find the answer to this and many other questions.

You are brave to want to venture into the unknown. I doubt there are many men so brave as you. God watched the man's head turn as he looked toward the open sea.

One day we will find out what is out there, he said pointing to the ocean. *And then another day we will find out what is out 'there'.* And his arm and finger shot up toward the sky.

I don't think I've ever met a man like you, God said. He looked at Naomi and she seemed to concur. Then he looked carefully at the man and with no further ado said, *Sir, can Naomi and I join you? We have walked for many many years and have seen much of the world. We too have wondered if there is more...if there is more world, different creatures, new places, new people, and new minds. Dear sir, we could work on your ship. We could help prepare the food for you and your men. We could help with the cleaning and the washing of your raiment.*

The man looked at God and Naomi, their tattered

clothes, and their serene faces. *But who are you?* he asked. *Where do you come from? How long have you been walking?*

I am God and this is Naomi. We come from afar where once the Jews and Romans cohabitated. But we left a very long time ago. We have been walking the earth for hundreds of years…

The man wondered if he was talking to a chimera. He had never heard such a voice of peace and serenity. *Do you know anything about boats and sailing the sea?*

We have little experience with water, but we have much experience with life. We have been on the earth for about fifteen hundred years.

The man's face lit up with a smile. He wondered if God and Naomi were mad or simpletons. But for some reason he was touched and his curiosity picqued.

So, my good fellow, why did you call yourself God?

Because that is the name my father and mother gave me.

And who are your father and mother?

Jesus Christ and Mary Magdalene, the most wonderful mother and father a man has ever had.

The man began laughing and he gently tapped God on the shoulder. But he could not refuse such kindness. He even imagined that he might need such people on the boat…imaginative people, perhaps slightly crazy, but people with no fear and nothing to lose, people who might amuse him and the other sailors. He thought for a moment and said, *Yes, my friends, you can come with us. We plan to leave in one month's time. So come back after thirty suns have risen and fallen. I will have a place for you on the boat.*

We will be here. We are as grateful for you as we are for life...

The ship's captain watched them turn and walk away arm in arm.

TEN

During the next four weeks God and Naomi often wondered if they would ever return to their known world again. And they thought more and more about death. Though any thinking person knows death is possible every minute of every day, we can go long stretches of our lives without a thought of dying. Then suddenly, for whatever reason death can become an obsession. What is it? Is it definitive? Might death just be another phase of life? Though God and Naomi had lived for nearly fifteen centuries – longer than any other human or animal on earth – they too had periods when they thought little about the subject. But as the days clicked away toward their departure, they felt death like burnt skin…

Naomi, we soon might never see any of this again.

Yes, God. Not only might we never see any of this

again, we soon might not see any of anything again.

Ah, dying, my love, is the greatest mystery of all…

Haven't you often said that there are two great mysteries: death and love.

I have often said that everything is a mystery (God chuckled as if he had just retold a worn-out joke and waved his arms at the sky). But yes…you are right…For me death and love are two of the subjects that have kept my mind spinning the most.

Is that what minds do…spin?

I have no idea. Can you think of a better word?

Trot?…gallop?…waltz?…wander?…fly like birds?… slither like snakes?…buzz like bees?…My dear God, I have no idea how a mind works, what pushes it on, what happens when death strikes…It too is a great mystery.

That is one reason why I've always thought dying will be interesting… We'll finally get to see if the mind lives on in some form or another.

Or we won't get to see that…

Yes, my love…Anyway, there are enough mysteries in life to keep even the vainest man humble and the most intelligent man in a state of wonder…

Let's hope this boat will take us to a new world, where we can live and love a little bit more…

In any case, before they left they tried to taste, feel, see, and touch as much of their known world as they could. They sucked the juice from oranges and lemons. They stared at flowers and examined their petals. They climbed hills and visited castles. They caressed cats, sheep, goats, and dogs. They watched birds and butterflies glide and bounce through the air. They sipped wine and ate tomatoes, cheeses, eggplant, potatoes, bread, and olives. Whenever God put an olive in his mouth he thought of his mother.

Naomi, do you remember my mother?

I only saw her for one day, but she left me a memory for a thousand years.

And to think she died that night we slept together for the first time…in her bed. It is a beautiful thought: she died in my bed while we were making love in hers.

You were so lucky to have had such a mother. I'm glad I saw her, even for only a day.

Yes… The other day I was thinking… I have observed myself for so many years I have come to an evident conclusion: I am happiest when two conditions are present… First, when my state of mind is that it is impossible to make sense of the world; that the world – and all existence – is so much of a great mystery, that it is ridiculous to think we could ever understand why one thinks what one does. That we can never understand what causes what because everything goes back too far, and yet at the same time be so grateful that anything exists at all… And the second condition is that I must be with the woman I truly love... Before it was my mother and now it is you… God's eyes filled with tears of joy.

Naomi covered God's face with kisses. *And I feel*

much the same thing....

They were both quiet for a long moment and for whatever reason, God said, *I wonder why the Jews and Christians think the world needs to be redeemed?...Redeemed from what? I would say the only redeemer in this world is love...true love...love like ours...and Jesus and Mary's. Only love can pull us above the tragedy of the human condition... not just the human condition...but the condition of all creatures...and all things...all things that are stuck in the quicksand of existence...I've said it many times before and I'll say it again...Nothing can be other than what it is...And love is the only way of breaking free. In love one's being is mixed with another's. In love one becomes two and two become one. That is the only freedom I know.*

And when I think that my parents never found real love on this earth, it greatly saddens me.

There is much to be sad about, my love...but there is as much to cause us to rejoice.

I would not have known it had I not met you, God.

Naomi's and God's eyes met through a double veil of tears. One can only cry so much in this world. There is a limit to the amount of pain and sadness one can feel. And there is only so much joy one can have before the mind and body explode. Tears of tragedy are best shed alone. Tears of love must be shared.

ELEVEN

The four weeks had nearly passed. Soon the great ship would be leaving. God and Naomi decided to write a letter…a letter to "Life". They used a mixture of languages that they had picked up over the centuries. Translated correctly into English, it went like this:

Dear Life,

In a few days we will be venturing into the unknown with about thirty other men. We will head in the direction of the setting sun, into the vast empty sea, hoping to find out how big our world is, if it is round or flat, and if there are other kinds of living things upon it. We have seen much; we hope to find more. We are well aware that we may never return to "this" world. We may be sucked into the ocean. We may disappear. We may die and drift into the other great unknown...

Before we go, we just want to thank you – life – for existing. You are the miracle of miracles, the greatest wonder of all. Every day we rejoice at the fact that there is something and not nothing.

As we may not come back, we would like to leave a few thoughts for all the human beings on this earth, all you creatures that share the blessing – and sometimes the curse – of language:

First, friends, when all is said and done, you should admit, once and for all, that you have no idea who and what you are. You think you know, but you don't. We have observed that most of you think you were created by some grand all-powerful God, and this thought gives your life value and meaning. But we want to tell you it is very possible that there is no such Being. The only real God we have encountered in our fifteen hundred years on earth is a man named "God", a man of flesh, blood, and bones like all of you – a man who may die soon. Most of you think Jesus was the Son of God. But no, this man was the son of Jesus Christ and Mary Magdalene and they named him "God". Jesus's parents were human and my parents were human...as human these thirty brave men with whom we are going into the unknown. God never knew his father Jesus. Jesus died an absurd death on a wooden cross months before God was born. But God lived with his mother Mary for eighteen years. She told him many times that she and Jesus gave him the name "God" such that the world would be sure to have at least one "real" god.

So, let us ask this question: if we, the people of this earth, are not the children of a divine god, then what are we? Do we have any idea? We think we do not. We are convinced that all existence is a great mystery. No one knows where the world came from. No one knows how anything got here. We have walked far and wide, certainly farther and wider than any other people. We have seen people of all kinds. We have listened, observed, and walked beside millions. And we have found that essentially nobody asks one crucial question… *"And what if there is no God? What then? What are we…really?"* Yes, what are we really? And if we are honest, we have no idea. We have our traditions and our various prophets and wise men. We tend to be satisfied with their answers. But after what we have observed all over the known world, we fear that all our explanations are mistaken. Let us be clear, there is nothing wrong with being mistaken because these answers give people comfort and meaning. But, we ask, wouldn't it be a wonderful day – a day of great liberation – if just once we all climbed out of our caves of delusion and untruth and looked straight into the light of existence, raised our arms toward the infinite, and declared…"Dear universe, you are such a mystery…the grandest mystery of all!"?

If and when someone finds this message, perhaps people will finally have stopped believing in the Christian God, the Islamic God, the Jewish God, and all the other gods. And when they do, they will stop saying that God created the universe and mankind. But we fear they will replace one explanation with another. We know that man's need for answers is so strong and we are afraid he will simply come up with a new idea about the origin of life. Perhaps he will start saying that he is the summit of some great "process"…some grand "becoming"…that has left man on top of the totem pole. He will then declare himself to be the highest creature. And then he will say that he and only he can "know the truth" about where we came from. He will continue to subtly look down on other creatures and see the rest of nature as somehow inferior to himself…somehow of "lesser" value and importance. And in a sense he will be right, for man is superior to other creatures in his ability to do certain things. But he forgets that other creatures can do things he can't do. No man can fly like an eagle. No man can smell like a dog. No man can jump like a cat. Yes, man excels in his ability to build objects like shoes and ships, but he is also the king of killing. He is far superior to other creatures in his ability to destroy life. He is perhaps the most powerful creature, but that does not make him the best creature. If anything, it makes him perhaps the most immoral creature. By seeing himself to be outside of nature – above nature – he pretends he wears a moral crown. But we fear he will never know what good and evil are because he does not know what reality is…

But we believe that a great day will come. We don't know when, but we think that finally man will realize - and openly admit - that he has absolutely no idea who and what he is – or, for that matter, what anything else is. He will stand in awe at the absolute mystery of Being. We believe this will be the greatest moment on earth, the moment when man finally becomes truly humble and is finally able to see himself in the mirror of reality. It will be the moment when man is truly "good", the moment when mankind begins to respect all existence, the moment from which mankind can move forward past its silly visions of history wherein it puts itself at the "center" of things.

Friends, we believe there is no center. We believe existence didn't "come" from anywhere, was not created by anyone, does not have a goal or a reason or logic. Existence simply is. And it is beautiful and amazing… Perhaps you who are reading this have come to agree us. We are sure you will be wonderful people.

So now, as we prepare to sail away with Captain Colon and his brave men, we want to thank you again, "life", for being there. We want to tell you that we accept your inscrutability, we accept the fact that every moment of existence is shrouded in mystery.

And we thank you for the other great mystery – love – which, in our case, has kept us from going crazy in this stupendous world.

Now, as we finish this letter, we hear your deep silence. Ah! you are in us and we are in you, somehow together… Forever?

Love, God and Naomi

They put the letter in an old clay pot and buried it in an olive grove near the Spanish port of Palos.

TWELVE

The next day God and Naomi went to the port where the majestic boat was sitting on the water like a floating mountain. All was abustle. Captain Colon was shouting orders and his men were scurrying about like ants. Naomi and God were told to help the group of eight men who were loading the food into the hull. Given that they had no idea how long they would be at sea and whether or not they would find food out there, they packed as much as they could. Colon, like God, thought there was a very good chance that the world was shaped like an apple and that it was possible for them to get to the other side of the world – to some of the places God and Naomi had visited – by going west instead of east. But nobody was sure and nobody knew how far they might have to go or how long it might take.

(We tend to forget how long the world existed before humans went all the way around it. What was the age of the earth – and mankind – when Magellan finally made the full circle? Ask a human being and he or she will give you a number. Ask the universe and it will give you a wink and a smile.)

The next morning they said goodbye to the world they knew. Other than the captain and God and Naomi, most of the crew members were criminals who had been given the choice between prison or a voyage into the unknown. The trip could have been quite a problem for Naomi (and God) given that she was the only woman on board. In spite of her one thousand five hundred years of living, she still had the charm of an unwithered rose. Captain Colon, understanding the potential explosiveness of the situation, informed the crew that immediate death would be the punishment for any man that laid a finger on Naomi. Hence, she and God were able to travel in relative peace. In fact, as they were responsible for the preparation and distribution of food, everyone wanted to stay on their good side.

As the days passed Naomi and God were awestruck by the humanity and bestiality of the crew. They saw incredible courage, strength, and comprehension as they watched the men fight together against high winds and treacherous seas. And then, when there was little wind and nothing to do, they saw despair, fear, sometimes weakness and jealousy. They saw some of the roughest men become peacemakers when fights broke out on board. When the fights were finished, the loser would often cower like a frightened mouse in a corner of the deck while the victor stared at the emptiness before them with the eyes of a sphinx.

One thing was certain: Captain Colon played the role of almighty leader and nobody seemed interested in taking his place.

After five weeks of generally favorable winds, they spotted land. They did not cheer or gloat as we might think, but rather stood next to the railing and gazed ahead with frozen eyes. What would they find? Should they prepare for war or peace? At least there was firm land and it was getting nearer by the second.

There were people on the sand. Human beings much like themselves were waiting for them. Colon told everyone to be on their guard, but to be as calm as possible…and to do nothing until he gave the order.

The people on the beach waved them ashore. Colon and four other men got in a small boat and went to greet them. Colon and the local chief talked, but naturally neither said anything that made any sense to the other. But all was peaceful, and with sign language it became clear that Colon and his group were welcome to anchor the boat and come on land. One of history's most incredible moments passed with astonishing ease and fluidity. What happened in the decade that followed was an entirely different story.

God and Naomi had enjoyed the experience on the

boat and had deeply appreciated the crew's hospitality, but they didn't want to continue with them. They yearned to immediately go off on their own and explore this new land. The day after their arrival, they thanked Colon and hugged each of the men. Then off they went again, hand in hand, into the "New World".

They quickly saw that it really wasn't new at all. It was simply a bit different. The people had arms and legs, heads and hair, noses and mouths, fingers and toes, age and youth, and language. What struck them most was the calm and kindness of these new humans. Rarely had they been greeted and treated so warmly.

After a few months of wandering, they realized they were on a rather large island, but an island nonetheless. Was this island the end of land and people? Was there more out there? As soon as they were able to understand the language, they were told that there was "more...much more", and fingers were pointed in various directions. More land was evidently not too far to the north, west, and even the south.

God and Naomi were happy to see that these people seemed to say nothing about the Jehovah, Jesus, the Virgin Mary, or any of the "prophets" and "commandments" in the Bible. None of that meant anything to them. They did however, seem to have a slew of other gods and explanations, which of course came as no surprise to God and Naomi. Once they watched strong men and leaders get into two small boats and head off to sea. Within a few days they were back with hulls full of fruits bursting with color and flavor that they had never seen or tasted before.

God and Naomi were happy with these people until, a few years later, Captain Colon returned to the island with more sailors, soldiers, and a group of so-called missionaries. God and Naomi were astounded to see that suddenly the Christian religion was being forced into the heads of these people. They were merciless; if the local people did not accept what the missionaries told them, they were threatened or killed. Many were taken into slavery and forced to look for gold or to build things for the Spaniards. They saw men being forced into the boats and taken back to Spain. What had been a placid world was being turned into torment and appalling violence. God and Naomi could not believe their eyes and abhorred what they saw, despite the fact that they had seen such horror and gore before in other parts of the world. But here, in this tropical paradise of sorts, it was shocking to behold. They tried to reason with the soldiers and missionaries by explaining that these people were kind and good and perfectly entitled to a different way of life. But it did no good. The Spanish invaders (and invaders they were) were sure of their god and they wanted gold. Most of them had not a grain of respect for the lifestyle of the native people. In fact, the word "people" is probably incorrect when describing how the Spaniards felt about the indigenes. "Animals" is far more appropriate, for they were treated as such. God and

Naomi cringed as they observed the spectacle of human dogmatism, intolerance, greed, and flat-headedness. They could do nothing to prevent it and wanted to get off the island as quickly as possible. They were finally able to gain passage on a boat whose captain assured them that they would be transported to another "terra firma" within two or three days.

He had told the truth. As soon as they were close to land they thanked the captain, jumped off the ship and swam to the shore. There was not a soul in sight. After drying off on a lovely golden beach, they wandered inland meeting only animals – alligators, bats, monkeys, opossums, mongooses, huge butterflies, moths, and snakes. They thought that perhaps this land was devoid of people…a new Garden of Eden, and they (they jokingly said) were Adam and Eve. For a few months they lived with the animals and survived on pineapples and, of course, their love.

They kept moving. Were there other people? They didn't count the days or nights, but eventually, they encountered a group of human beings. They looked much like the people Naomi and God had lived with on the island, though their language was quite different. They, too, were very kind and lived a simple existence. Their houses had no real walls, but were platforms attached to poles under ceilings of palm branches. They slept above the ground and out of the reach of crawling creatures.

Naomi and God decided not to stay, but to keep exploring. Slowly but surely they met many different groups, but rarely did they stay long enough to learn the new languages. Often they would walk for many weeks alone. All the people they encountered tended to be calm and seemed satisfied with their lot in life. None seemed bent on belligerence. Like the islanders before the arrival of the missionaries, it was obvious that none of these societies had any notion whatsoever of a Christian God, and there was no parading of God's father Jesus agonizing on the cross. Understanding what they could, they remarked that nobody ever seemed to talk about guilt, sin, heaven or hell. God imagined that his father would have appreciated these people. Many groups used the words "Wakan Tanka" to talk about their feeling about life. From what they could garner, it meant something like "The Great Mystery". These human beings also seemed to respect animals as much as people. In some ways it seemed that they saw animals to be superior to people given that they could do things people couldn't do like fly and glide above the world, or run and jump much faster and higher than men. In fact, it eventually became clear than some of their gods were beautiful creatures from their jungles and forests.

One night as Naomi and God were falling asleep, they had this conversation:

How much longer do you want to keep walking?

I don't know. But I am enjoying these people.

However, I fear for them. I can feel the winds of change.

Which winds do you mean? Some winds are pleasant and cooling, whereas others are fierce and knock down trees and destroy villages.

The latter, my love. I fear that the Spanish – and others from across the sea – will come here in large numbers and little by little they will destroy these people.

You mean like what we saw before on that first island?

Yes. I can feel the land beneath our feet will one day be completely different. This part of the world will look like that other part of the world. We have seen it everywhere. The powerful eat the weak. And they always take control in the name of their god. We have witnessed it over and over.

But these people here do not seem to want to take over the weak. They appear satisfied with what they have. They don't speak of gold and riches and conquering.

And that is why I fear they will disappear – because their vision of life is "not" one of superiority and conquest. They respect animals as much as each other. They respect the sun, the moon, the earth, the trees, the fish, the alligators, and even the snakes that flee the sound of their feet. They do not want to dominate other creatures. They want to live with them. Colon and his people want gold, mammon, and aggrandizement.

They see other creatures only in terms of what they can do to help them enrich themselves.

You know God, in general I prefer these people to the ones on the other side of the great ocean. Their eyes seem to be open wider. Their hearts are bigger. Their heads hold less hatred.

And from what we have seen so far, they do not massacre in the name of a god. They do not conquer in the name of a god. They do not threaten in the name of a god…We saw on the other side of the sea how the people build more, expand more, and simply seem to want more, including a trip to heaven after they die. These people want less. They are more satisfied with what they have. Their needs are minimal. But this will be their downfall. They will perish when the Spanish come in greater numbers and with guns and weaponry. One needn't be a visionary to see this.

Naomi and God talked no more that night. Time stopped. The world froze. They fell asleep in each other's arms.

THIRTEEN

One might ask how God and Naomi were able to travel so long together and not "explode" as a couple. (Even my dear conservative mother said that a couple should "travel" together before getting married as it was the only real way to see if people were truly compatible. God and Naomi took her advice to heart.) Didn't they fight? Didn't they get on each other's nerves? Didn't they get tired of each other's company after fifteen centuries together? … No, they didn't, for the simple reason they had really become one person. Their minds and bodies had woven together such that neither felt whole without the other. Once they realized this, there was no longer the question of whether or not they loved each other, because they were love. They had fused into one mind, one body, one love, much like two streams come together at the foot of the mountain to make a lake or a pond. This happens very rarely on earth with human beings. But like a mother and a baby inextricably linked in the womb, so God and Naomi were one. The cosmos was their womb. Naomi's mind was inside God's mind; God's mind was inside hers. Their beings had fused… But let us be clear: We are not arguing that this is necessarily a good thing. Perhaps, for some, it is better to be a lone wolf in the forest. Perhaps sometimes solitude is preferable to love. But in the case of Naomi and God, real love had become a reality. If clouds, water, and atoms can fuse, there is no reason why people can't. Without the fusion of hydrogen and oxygen, there would be no life on earth. Without the fusion of God and Naomi this story would never have been told, and forgotten.

Of course, in the beginning, like all couples, they had had their little moments of fear and jealousy. When you love like they loved each other, you tend to think that the whole world loves the other person the way you do. When you are apart, you think every member of the opposite sex will fall in love with your paramour just like you did. You see everyone as a potential enemy who might steal your beloved. You are enveloped by fear. You tremble like Kierkegaard who thought no human relation could ever be trusted, could ever be permanent, stable, fixed. For Kierkegaard, only a relationship with God could be solid and forever… Well, that's what happened – Naomi had her God, Kierkegaard had his. They were different Gods, of course, but the result was the same: true love lasting for as long as eternity does.

God and Naomi came to realize quite early that all the problems they had between each other simply came from – and were because of – their deep and abiding love. Every negative feeling or emotion for the other (the jealousy, the fear of loss) was because of their love. They came to understand that it was silly to bicker about things that might threaten their love, but which, in the end, only confirmed it. Once they understood – like the great sage Winnie-the-Pooh – that "it all comes from loving honey so much", God and Naomi's union was never menaced again.

FOURTEEN

After decades of watching the conquest and annihilation in the area that is today called Central America, Naomi and God had had enough. They hoped for one thing: that they would never witness horror on such a massive scale again. But they were disappointed. There was much more to come.

Fortunately, as is seemingly always the case on earth, they did not only witness cruelty, greed, destruction, suffering, and slaughter, but they also saw many acts of kindness, tenderness, and goodness of heart. The world is never all bleakness. There are always acts of understanding, compassion, contemplation, and warmth on all sides of the fence. God and Naomi were spectators to some of the worst atrocities ever to befall the human race, but they also saw sharing, sacrifice, creation, hope, love, and joy.

The world always has many faces. Sometimes they wondered if there wasn't, in fact, a strange hidden balance of things? Is there a kind of equilibrium to what goes on in life? For every act of cruelty is there an act of kindness? Somehow the world continues to function. Is existence a stream of opposites struggling and pushing each other onward? Is life a dialectic of some kind? Is one man's success always another man's failure? Do joy and pain exist in equal proportions? Are the scales balanced when it comes to loving and hating? Then again perhaps these terms were all human inventions which, in the end, had nothing to do with anything real – nothing to do with the blood and guts of life. They asked themselves, *What is a civilization? When does such a thing start? When does it end? Does it start when the first person dreams or sets up his or her tent? Does it end when the last person dies? Perhaps Egypt never really started and never really disappeared. And Rome? It's still there. It's still on the map...centuries and centuries after it 'fell'...* Human beings love to lay out the pieces of the puzzle on a big flat table and then put them together to make a neat clean whole picture. They love to make sense of things. But God and Naomi had come to see that the world is not a puzzle that can be broken into bits and pieces. It is one continuous flow – one great river, one enormous ocean of life and death, coming and going, appearing and disappearing. Jesus had flowed into the Jews and the Romans and the man Paul. The Christian river flowed into Islam which flowed into the Dark Ages and Middle Ages. Captain Colon built his boats and sailed west, and then…and then…and then… The world does not stop. It is an eternal flow of water, land, flesh, blood, and brain. Nothing is pure. There are no pure people, pure thoughts, pure principles, or pure races. Time cannot be cut up. Events cannot be separated. The ocean of humanity is no different than the ocean of the world. There is no dividing line between the oceans. It is all one body of water. All is linked. People who try to break history into pieces and weave their tapestries of truth and hang them on the walls of the great halls of knowledge are all mistaken. None has the true picture.

God and Naomi walked and wondered. Of all the humans they had observed in the world, which group was the most open to life, to others, to feeling and understanding, to man's proper place in the world? But did man have a proper place? Were the people who were destroyed by the Spaniards in their proper place? Didn't the Spaniards think that they were in their proper place? Would the Spaniards be gone too one day? Don't all civilizations eventually disappear only to be misunderstood and falsely judged by posterity?

For two years they walked south on an isthmus that would take them to another huge continent where another great civilization was prospering, only to soon be partially annihilated. They knew it was only a matter of time until enough boats crossed the ocean from the east – boats loaded with guns, bibles, and diseases. And that time had already arrived. The soldiers and missionaries were already climbing ashore. These native inhabitants too would soon see much of their world shattered. Power is like a tsunami whose only justification is itself. But men like to mix morality with power. The formula is simple: the Portuguese and Spaniards called themselves "good" and what they conquered was "evil" and "inferior".

One spring day they sat down near a river to drink and rest. A crocodile swam by. Then another. Neither was hungry and God and Naomi were not bothered or frightened. They stretched out on the ground and soon were sleeping. They were awakened by an enormous snake that was crawling over their warm bodies. They remained still and let it slither. It let them be. It had just finished digesting a small monkey and God and Naomi were of no more interest than a rock or a tree. When it was gone Naomi said, "I used to be afraid of snakes." "We have seen many. Now we know what to expect." "In general, if you leave them alone, they do the same to you." "So it is with most people." "I often try to imagine what goes on in the mind of a snake. How does it think? What is real for it? How does it perceive us? If no words go through its head, how does it make sense of us…and the world?" "I don't know. Perhaps it is too intelligent for words and concepts and has no use for them. It might be that it comprehends existence in a way we can't." "Do we understand how 'we' comprehend?" "Sometimes I think we, too, just slide and glide through life...over land and over people...never really knowing or understanding what we touch." "Yesterday I was petting a cat and I wondered what the connection between the two of us really was. How closely could we feel each other?" "It would seem that we never know." They stayed on the riverbank until the world darkened and the moon appeared. "Do you think the moon is moving? Maybe we are moving? It would make just as much sense to say that the earth is moving as to say the moon is moving." "Perhaps both are moving, like two people crossing each other on a path." "Might the path not be moving, too?" "If what we are standing on is moving, maybe what is under what we are standing on is moving, too." "And what if everything is moving all the time?" "Will we ever know?" "And I wonder about all the parts that are moving in my head and body...the ones that make me see, hear, feel, think, talk, walk, and desire to be with you." "It's all part of the mystery." "The mystery that so few seem to feel..." "Do you think the snake that crawled across our bodies feels it?" "What?" "The mystery." "I don't know, but I doubt it. If there is one thing that separates creatures, it is the ability to sense the unknown." "Yes. That...and the capacity to love." "Don't you think greatest lovers feel the greatest mystery?" "Yes, those who feel the greatest mystery are capable of the greatest love." "Can we be sure?" "No." "What are you sure of?" "Love and mystery. The rest slips away like water on the skin of a snake."

FIFTEEN

They walked along the coast as far south as they could. Then they turned back northward. A hundred years passed. Two hundred. Much of the original population had been either killed or conquered. The people were mixing, but the light-skinned men had the power. They could be seen everywhere toting guns and telling people what to do. The autochthons were doing the hard labor, cutting trees, building houses, cultivating fields, and carrying the loads.

Naomi and God watched this flow of humanity. They flowed with it. They tried to imagine the life of every person they came in contact with. They knew there were limits to compassion. You can only care so much. You can only understand so much. The local people were being replaced by new local people. Perhaps thousands of years before the same process had gone on. Now, after a couple hundred years, Spanish and Portuguese were becoming indigenous. In any case, God's fears had become reality. The invaders had spread north, south, and west like blood oozing from a wound. The Lord God and His Son Jesus were constantly invoked, prayed to, feared, thanked, and worshipped.

The human God was walking with Naomi. As they got farther north they suddenly began to hear two new languages, French and English had come. These speakers too had come across the ocean. Their hair tended to be a bit lighter than the Portuguese and Spanish. But they too carried the guns and swords.

SIXTEEN

The years wore on. Nations were being formed. Constitutions were written. The people with the light skins were demanding independence from the kings and queens back on the other side of the ocean who were taxing them and demanding that they send back goods. Thousands of new slaves with deep purple-black skins were arriving in boats from afar. After almost eighteen hundred years of walking, God and Naomi arrived in a place that called itself "The United States of America". It was bustling, as masses of people were arriving from Europe trying to find what they called a better life. Who could argue with a creature that wanted to improve its lot? Of course few of these people thought about or understood how their better life meant a worse life for the native people. But humans have never been very insightful when it comes to seeing the other side of things.

Slowly but surely this new country was split and a vicious internal war broke out. For once, the newcomers were not killing the indigenous people, but had taken to slaughtering each other. Naomi and God watched in horror as young men were thrown into the battle, maiming each other with bullets and bayonets. Again they observed how both sides swore that they had divine powers behind them and in their underpants. Blood and soiled sweat watered the earth for four gruesome years until finally the Southern side waved a white flag. The mess was cleaned up, the dead never came back, the charcoal-skinned slaves could no longer be owned. Soon after, the remaining "Indians" (as they'd been labeled) were herded onto – into – reservations. Yes, the slaves had been unchained, but that did not necessarily mean their lives were quickly made better. And the Indian reservations got smaller and smaller when the white man found gold on them, and, in the end, were usually located on the land the government and pioneers wanted the least.

But the powerful new nation continued to grow and expand to the west. God and Naomi wandered everywhere. They were shocked to see that fifty years after the Civil War, in many parts of the country the dark-skinned people still could not use the same toilets, drink the same water, or go to the same restaurants, hotels, and schools as the Caucasians.

Again, they were fascinated that a people who professed to be followers of Jesus could be so blockheaded and downright obtuse. They were no longer shocked by such nonsense as they had seen it in so many places. And when these "Americans" – as they called themselves – commenced to claiming they were "God's country" and "the greatest nation on earth", God and Naomi could only chuckle, especially since many of the people had never been to another land. But otherwise, they tended to be rather happy and jolly people, happy to have found their promised land. They watched cars and airplanes be invented, factories sprouting up everywhere, roads and airports built, hospitals and schools blossoming wherever people congregated in mass. At one point, the entire country turned into a great machine for making military equipment and preparing hundreds of thousands of new young men for battle. For the second time the European continent had turned into a human slaughterhouse. God and Naomi were relieved to be "here" and not there. They had seen enough killing.

While all this was going on, they decided to walk through every state from sea to shining sea. For the next thirty years they went to the national parks, big cities, deserts, small towns, forests, monuments, mountains, valleys, and fields. They saw Bryce Canyon in summer, the Grand Canyon at sunrise, Montana, North Dakota, Mississippi, Louis Armstrong singing "What a Wonderful World in New Orleans, Tennessee,

Nebraska, the Boston Garden, the streets of San Francisco, the Empire State building, the ghettoes of Harlem, Detroit, and Oakland, and they were even on hand when the first Disneyland opened in the middle of the orange groves of Anaheim in the mid-1950s. They didn't miss the last Beatles concert in Candlestick Park, nor did they ignore Death Valley, Yuma, Yankee Stadium, Caesar's Palace, Moonlight Ranch, Salt Lake City, the Tabernacle Choir, the Playboy Mansion, Chinatown, Denny's in Denver, the Boeing factory, the Seahawks, Chicago, Nashville, Memphis, Elvis, Fred Astaire dancing across a ceiling, the Black Panthers, John Kennedy shot in Dallas, Dr. King murdered, Bobby Kennedy's dead body on a kitchen floor in Los Angeles, Sandy Koufax pitching in Dodger Stadium, or the Rose Bowl parade in Pasadena, the beauty of Bill Russell and Wilt Chamberlain loping down the court, the Great Lakes, Niagara Falls, and New York Knicks winning the NBA crown.

Finally, after more than a hundred years of meandering through forty-eight states (they never made it to Alaska or Hawaii), on July 4th, 1973 they arrived at the Nation's Capital in Washington, D.C.

SEVENTEEN

Actually they cheated a little and had taken a train down from New York. Two-thousand-year-olds deserve a break. When people asked them how old they really were, God would say, "I'm one thousand nine hundred and seventy-three, but she's four years younger." But the truth is, God was never entirely sure how old they were. Of course at this point it didn't really matter. He had never understood exactly how the Western world was keeping track of time with their B.C. and A.D. stuff. It seemed they used B.C. on one side of his father and A.D. on the other side. As far as he knew, B.C. meant "Before Christ", but A.D.… what did that mean? If it meant "After the Death of Jesus", then he was 1,973 exactly years old. But other people told him that A.D. actually meant "Anno Domini" which he knew (from his days of speaking Latin) meant something like "in the year of our Lord". This Anno Domini A.D. started keeping time from Jesus's birth, which would tack an extra thirty-three years onto his life. This made a lot more sense than the "After Death" idea, which would render the thirty-three years of Jesus's life as having never happened, at least on the calendar, and of course would make God thirty-three years younger. He knew that in the great scheme of things none of this really mattered an iota, nor did it tell us anything whatsoever about the actual age of the earth or the universe.

Be that as it may, God and Naomi had every right to be tired after some twenty centuries on earth and the hundreds of thousands of kilometers that had passed under their feet. They reckoned they deserved that train ride down the east coast from New York.

They got to Union Station at nine-thirty in the evening, just as darkness was falling. It was the train's last stop and all the passengers descended. God and Naomi were struck by the relative silence in the cavernous station. Nobody was waiting on the platform to greet anybody and none of the arriving passengers expressed any joy upon meeting their destination. The herd scuttled away, the sound of footsteps echoing as people lethargically made their way toward the exits.

When Naomi and God got outside, the summer air had a slightly metallic smell and felt like it stuck on their skin. As always, they had no idea where they were nor where they were going. They hadn't used a map for two millennia and they weren't about to start then. They began to wander down a large street. Both now limped and their gait was slow. They got to an intersection (Massachusetts Avenue and 2nd St. NE, but they didn't know it) and stopped to rest. Two young men approached them hurriedly. God noticed that one man had a knife in his hand, so he smiled and started the conversation:

Good evening gentlemen. Are you going to a dinner party? Do you have a steak or turkey to carve?

Yo, muthafuggas. We ain gah no time fo no bullshittin…Empty yo fuggin poggets.

I beg your pardon, sir. God and Naomi were normally quite good with languages. They spoke over a hundred of them and knew English quite well. But they were having trouble understanding the young man. *I'm sorry,* God said, *but I do not understand your words.*

Ah sezz gimme yo gawd dam fuggin cash rih now o weez gunna cut you mutha fuggers up. The taller man put the knife closer to God's body wanting to make sure that the old man saw the lustrous blade.

Did I hear you correctly? Did you say "God"? How did you know my name? It's a pleasure to meet you. What is your name?

Yo, Slim, we don give a gawddamm fugg who yo azzes be, we jus wants yo money. Under the street light sweat balls glistened on his ebony brow.

There you go again using my name. Thank you for your politeness. Are we to understand that you are having financial problems? We have observed that many people have financial problems here in your country. Many people in many other parts of the world share your fate…

Yo professa…we ain gah no time ta be talkin' bout no fuggin state uh da gawd damm wuld…

I am like my father…Jesus. You might have heard of him yourself … He gave everything he had to the poor. He would give his shoes or the shirt off his back if another man needed it.

Ah don giv a fugg who yo daddy be and wez don need no fuggin clothes…and wez gah plenia shooz…

I see, kind sir, but I must tell you that Naomi and I have not had money for almost two thousand years.

Wha da fugg!…Ain had no money fo how long? You shu be da wuns shuh be fuggin robbin us! The two men looked at each other laughed.

My dear friends…What are your names?

Yo…Gawd…dat yo name, ain it?…Yuz gotz ta be wunna da funniest sunzzabitches ize evah seen. Ha ole you say yo azz iz?

Approximately one thousand nine hundred and seventy-three years old. It might depend on who's counting.

Gaw damm…I canst even coun da fuggin far…

I must correct you. My last name is not Damn. I normally don't use a last name. But if you insist, Christ would be mine.

Yo name be Gaw Christ! Holy fugg!!! Yo...listen man... Ah gots a serius queshun fo ya...Whe yo azz live? He motioned to his friend to put the knife away.

We just live on the earth. We have no home. We have been walking all over the world for almost two thousand years. We originally left Palestine when my mother died and when Naomi's father beat her severely because she wouldn't marry the man he had chosen for her.

Nah ain dat sum shiiit...leas she had a fuggin father. Ah ain neva see mine.

Listen, my friends, Naomi and I are very hungry and thirsty? Are you hungry? Maybe we could look for some food together. And why don't we go somewhere where we can sit down and talk? And at least have a glass of water

Yo Mustang... (he addressed his partner in life and crime)*... Iz thinkin' ma mudda wu luv ta mee dis muthafugga an his ole lady...*

Yo Tiga...Ah think yooz ri...

And so it came to pass that Anthony "Tiger" Taylor and Michael "Mustang" Jones took God and Mary on the cross-town bus to the southeast part of the city where Anthony's mother greeted them in her semi-rundown ghetto home. She was a wonderful woman with a heart the size of a coconut. She gave them food and a place to sleep. She was as kind and hospitable as anybody they had met on their voyage. While they were eating biscuits and sipping hot chocolate, she told God and Naomi about how she prayed to the Good Lord every night to keep her children out of jail… *"Ders anuf ghetto kiz in der…Dey don needs no mo. Ma boy Tony awready bin in der twice…an daz two time too many!"* Anthony was the oldest of her five children.

By the time they finished their snack, it was after midnight and it was apparent that Naomi and God were very tired. Mrs. Taylor took them to her bedroom. She gave them her bed and wouldn't hear to any other solution for the night's sleeping arrangements. She would be fine on the couch.

EIGHTEEN

Since her husband disappeared, Loretta Taylor works two jobs six days a week. She leaves at five in the morning for her job at the high school where she sweeps floors and washes windows until noon; then at one she hops a bus to Hamilton Hotel where she changes sheets, vacuums carpets, keeps things shiny. Before going to sleep that night with her guests, God and Naomi, she says, *So you fokes jus may yoseves ri at home. Ders plenny fo brefus in da frige an ders cereal in da cubud.*

Thank you. It's so kind of you to take us in like this. We won't stay long.

Ih ain evy day, I gets ta have a man named God in ma houz. Iz you relly two thousan yiz ol?

It's been a long road.

You dun musta seen a ho la in yo day.

We've seen a few things.

Okay…Iz gotsta ta ge up erly fo wuk. If dem kizz mess up tumaha, you spank der bottoms pink.

I'm sure they'll be fine. We might be gone before you get back…

You duze whah you wan. Bu yooz wecome to stay az long az you likes. Iz gotsta ge some sleep. Wuz nice meetin yall.

They hear her go out the door at five, but sleep for another two hours. When they get up and tiptoe downstairs to the kitchen, the rest of the house is silent. As they sip their coffee, the youngest, little Latisha staggers into the room with her teddy bear. She does not seem to be surprised to see the two strangers. She says good morning and turns on the TV. Cartoons fill the screen. A few minutes later Dontaye shows up and without a word installs himself next to his sister on the couch. He has a rag in his hand and puts a thumb in his mouth. He must be about eight. Naomi stands and offers the children juice and donuts that she has found in the refrigerator. Both decline with a wag of the head. A few minutes later, a hurricane floats down the stairs. As soon as he sets eyes on the strangers the whole atmoshere changes…

Who ah you? Wher you cum from? Yuz luh li misser and missus Muthuzala who be livin bout nih hured yir. He talks like a machine gun.

We came in last night with your brother Anthony. We met him on the street.

Ah beh he tri ta rob yo azz.

That might have been his original intention, but he ended up being a most pleasant fellow.

Wher you dun learn ta talk lak da?

It's not important. What might your name be?

Jerry. Da one an ony Jerry. All fo fee fo inches uh me. So I seez yuz met Tish and Dontaye.

Not really. But they're adorable children.

They ain ta much cuz thez kinna shy.

Jerry helps himself to a bowl of Wheaties. He sits down at the table with God and Naomi.

So howz you ge so old? Ah ha a grampa who gotz ta be bout niney-fl, bu you gah him be by a mile. Wher you cum from eyway?

We were in New York yesterday. We've been walking around the world for a long time.

Da wuld! Shi, I ain been outta D.C.

From what we hear, you have a lot of nice monuments here in the nation's capital.

Ya, bu I ain neva seen nun of em.

You haven't seen any of the monuments in Washington, D.C.?

Nope. Who gunna tay me? Sanna Claus? Ain nobuey gunna sho me no monaments here. Momma wuk ah day. I seen em on TV doh.

Jerry pours more milk on his cereal.

Now Jerry, how old are you?

Ten.

So you're in school...

Na now. Dis ih summa vacashun…but den we gah sku again.

What grade are you in?

Ah be starrin fi grade.

Fifth grade?

Yeah.

That's wonderful. Do you like school?

Ain do nuttin bu mez aroun…

God decides he will do a little social anthropology. They are in the nation's capital, probably only a few hundred meters from the Capitol Building itself. He will ask Jerry a few questions to see what he has learned so far in school. The boy obviously has a very quick mind.

Jerry, let me ask you a question or two. First, that milk you just poured on your cereal…where does it come from?

Fru da sto.

I know it comes from the store. But before it comes to the store, where is it made?

In a mil fatory.

It is made in a milk factory?

Wher da hell elz ih gunna be made?

Jerry, milk comes from cows.

Shiiiiiiii…mil don come fru no cow…

It really does. Maybe we can take you to a farm where you can see real cows.

Nobuey neva ta me nowher…I ain neva been ouside da neybahood.

You've never been outside of your neighborhood?
Nope.

God looks around the room for a pencil and a piece of paper. He finds both next to the telephone. *Okay Jerry. Here's a piece of paper and a pencil. Now I'm going to dictate a few sentences to you. You write down what I say. Okay, are you ready?*

Jerry doesn't say anything. He puts his spoon down, picks up the pencil and stares at the white piece of paper.

My…name…is…Jerry…I…live…in…Washington D. C.

Jerry's hand doesn't move.

Jerry, write what I say. This is just for fun. I'm not going to give you a grade or anything. MY…NAME…IS…JERRY…I…LIVE…IN…WASH…

Jerry looks at God.

Yo… Gawd. I ca ri nuttin. I ain neva learn howda ri.

You mean you're going into the fifth grade and you haven't learned to write.

No suh…

There is a hint of shame on Jerry's face.

Can you read?

I ca read needa.

You haven't learned how to read either?

Nah rilly

Jerry, what do you do in school all day? Don't you have books and exercises and things?

Wez ony ga a cuppla boo fo all da class…we don

do nuttin in sku…

Naomi looks at Jerry, then at his brother and sister curled up on the couch watching cartoons. These are real children with real lives. Anthony, the practicing delinquent, is still asleep upstairs. There is an older sister, too. None of these kids has asked to be born. None asked to be born where they were born. What will happen to them? What kind of lives will they have? She looks at God. They are both filled with love. What else can one be filled with when one sees such conditions? The whole world is innocent. They both know it. They have seen more of the world than any two people who have ever lived. Every single solitary drop of existence is as innocent as rain. The world turns and turns. How long has it been turning? Nobody knows. Nobody will ever know. Nothing in existence can know existence. But it isn't just the world that is turning. Everything is turning. Time, space, bodies, minds, atoms, planets, galaxies, clocks, generations, life, death. It is all innocent. Nothing asks to be what it is. All is virginal. This is the great lesson she and God have learned after two thousand years of existence. Things are what they are. Everything. The best to the worst. The happiest to the saddest. The most fortunate to the least fortunate. Nothing can stop the world. It will go where it will go. If people want to believe there is a grand god in the sky who loves and protects them, let them. In any case, they will believe what they believe. If Latisha and Dontaye want to sit on the couch all day and watch cartoons, let them…

Naomi is overcome by a great sadness, but also a great liberation. God looks at her. They both know what she is feeling. What can one do? She knows there is a better life than watching TV all day. She knows there is a better life than robbing innocent people in the street. She knows there is a better life than not being able to read or write at age ten. But what can she do? Can she educate these children? Should she and God spend the rest of their lives right there in Loretta Taylor's house trying to help these kids? She and God know they are going to die soon. Two thousand years has been enough. They have seen more and loved each other more than any two people in the history of the world. Can they really help these kids? Can they help Loretta Taylor? They could cook and clean while she works. They could educate the kids. But what does it mean to educate someone? Probably less than one kilometer from where they are is the building that houses the Congress of the United States of America, the most powerful nation in the world. It is filled with so-called educated men and women. But are they really educated? Are their lives better than any other lives? Are they happier? Don't they believe in all kinds of lies like justice, free will, God, history? Aren't most of the members of congress frustrated in their marriages? Don't they all want more? More money? More power? More votes? Bigger cars? Bigger houses? Another lover? Re-election? Headlines? Naomi thinks about the world. God is thinking with her. They sit at that table with Jerry. They put out their hands and touch each other's fingers. The touch of love. They love each other. They love Jerry, Dontaye, and Latisha. They love the world. They love existence. All of it. The whole glorious salmagundi. The whole heaven. The whole hell. The whole beauty. The whole monstrousness. In the end, isn't existence kind of an all or nothing deal? If it's all tied together, if there is no beginning and no end, if there is no real "history", if every moment is infinite, if nothing can be other than what it is, if the whole bag of marbles really is just there…forever and ever…then if one piece was gone, the whole thing would be gone.

As Naomi and God hold hands and look around the room, they think about all they have seen in those two thousand years. All the suffering, all the killing, one group controlling another, the armies, the inquisitions, the conquests, the slaves, the kings, the concubines, the Jews, the Romans, the Greeks, the Vietnamese, the Chinese, the Mongolians, the Turks, the Africans, the Spanish, the Indians, the Aztecs, Incas, Mayans, and the Americans. It is all one very slow-moving process. Life on this earth is one huge laborious snail that oozes through time and space, slowly, ever so slowly, moving from point A to point B. Here they are in the capital of great America and there are children in 1973 who can't read or write, children who have never been more than two miles from their home, children whose mother works twelve hours a day and whose older brother is a delinquent. The slaves that were taken from Africa are still here; their form had just changed. And aren't even the men and women across the park in the Capitol Building a different kind of slave? Aren't they slaves to their own pasts just like Jerry, Latisha, and Dontaye are slaves to theirs? They are slaves to their religions, their places, their positions, their values, their so-called principles.

The snail is eking its way across deserts and jungles, forests, mountains, valleys, oceans, cities. The living and the dead are everywhere.

God and Naomi join the latter group not long after their stay with Loretta Taylor and her family. They leave Washington, D. C. that morning around eleven and take a greyhound bus westward bound. They are too tired to walk any more. After three days of travel they are at the Grand Canyon. They want to see it one more time. From there they write a letter to Jerry Taylor:

Dear Jerry (and Loretta and family),

Thanks for letting us stay with you. We enjoyed every second of our visit. Jerry, we know you can't read this letter, but we want you to have your mother (or somebody else if she can't read) read it to you over and over and over until you can understand it and read it back to her. It could be a start to you having a better life. What is a better life? What is a good life? Though we have seen more of the world than any two people ever to have lived, we cannot answer these questions for you. Each person must respond for himself or herself. There are as many different answers as there are people on earth.

You come from the D.C ghetto. Your brother Anthony is already a criminal. He'll probably end up in prison or dead on a sidewalk. This is sad because he seems like he could be a very nice fellow. Maybe this letter might even help him…and his friend Mustang. We don't know. One never knows who or what one really helps. All you can do is try.

What we want to tell you, Jerry, is that it is very possible that you only have one life to live and then you die and are gone forever. People talk a lot about gods, Jesus, a resurrection, an afterlife, etc. We are sure you have seen those evangelist Christian pastors on television on Sunday morning. But Jerry, it is very probable that everything they say is a lie. No one knows for sure what happens when a person or an animal or anything dies.

Our hope is that you make the best of your time on earth, whatever that means. Don't just follow the crowd. Be Jerry. Be unique. We also suggest that, if possible, you try not to make life miserable or unpleasant for those around you. There is enough suffering and pain as it is. Just look at your mom and how hard she works. Would you want to make things any harder for her?

You're what? Ten years old Jerry? If you're lucky, you'll have another seventy years to do things. You're a very intelligent boy. You have a good strong body and a wonderful mind. Use that mind and your body. And, if possible, use them to love.

What is love? You'll have to find that out for yourself.

Jerry, from what we know life is a great mystery. You are part of that mystery. Those cows that make the milk you put on your Wheaties are also part of that mystery. Open your eyes. Try to smile at the world. It is all we have.

Thanks again and may Jerry bless Jerry,

Your friends, Naomi & God

After posting the letter at the lodge, they walk to the rim of the canyon. God climbs over the little guardrail first, then helps Naomi. Neither look down. They embrace. And then, hand in hand and their eyes locked, they step out.

The onlookers *ooh* and *aah* and many scream with horror. Of course, they have no idea what they are seeing.

JON FERGUSON

Jon Ferguson was born in October 1949 in Oakland, California, into a devout Christian family, much like his favorite philosopher, Friedrich Nietzsche. In fact, as a child, church services were held in the family living room. At age 17, his passion for sport was almost usurped by a keenness to save the world when he enrolled at Brigham Young University. Little by little, though, he realized that if Jesus couldn't do it, neither could he. His faith in divinity began to crumble. With an adieu to the US academic world where he'd been immersed in anthropology and philosophy – and with a desire to engage with the world at large – Ferguson hopped on a plane in 1973 and by chance ended up in Nyon, Switzerland where he was soon playing basketball in the top Swiss league, becoming a key player in what fans consider to have been the golden age.

Half a century later he is now just as well known for his writing (eighteen books published in French) as for his coaching (thirty years' worth). He won more games than any coach in Swiss basketball history, but he likes to remind people that he lost more than everyone else as well... He has written over twenty novels and a book on Nietzsche, Nietzsche au Petit Déjeuner ("Nietzsche for Breakfast") and a book on the history of Swiss basketball, Of Hoops and Men. For twenty-five years he also wrote a bi-weekly column in the Lausanne newspaper called "Ainsi Parla Schmaltz". His novel Farley's Jewel (Cinco Puntos Press, 1998) won a Barnes & Noble "Discover Great New Writers of America" prize.

Sign up for his publisher's newsletter at
www.jonfergusonbooks.com

Have you enjoyed *God & Naomi*? Let us know by emailing
editor@hugejam.com

BOOKS BY JON FERGUSON

(Published by Huge Jam, 2022)

Adam's Cane
Foster's Depression
The Last Day Forever
Jesus & Mary
Mary & God
God & Naomi

Download 'The Last Day Forever' for free from the author's website
www.jonfergusonbooks.com

Out soon by the same author:

The Old Man and the Stone
Farmer's Daughter
Don't Bullshit Me Daddy
The Anthropologist

www.hugejam.com
www.jonfergusonbooks.com